5-MINUTE STAR WARS STORIES

Disney • LUCASFILM PRESS

PRESS

LOS ANGELES • NEW YORK

Collection © & TM 2015 Lucasfilm Ltd.

"Race to the Finish Line," "Yoda and the Count," and "The Last Adventure" written by Rebecca L. Schmidt

"Escape from Darth Vader" written by Brooke Dworkin and illustrated by Stephane Roux

"Destroy the Death Star!" written by Trey King

"The Battle of Hoth" written by Calliope Glass

"A Jedi, You Must Become" written by Andy Schmidt and illustrated by Stephane Roux and Pilot Studio

"Rescue from Jabba's Palace" and "The Ewoks Join the Fight" written by Brooke Dworkin

"A Friend for Rey" and "Rathtars on the Loose!" written by Elizabeth Schaefer

Unless otherwise noted, all illustrations by Pilot Studio

Printed in the United States of America

First Edition, December 2015

10 9 8 7 6 5 4 3 2 1

FAC-038091-15306

Library of Congress control number on file.

ISBN 978-1-4847-2820-8

SUSTAINABLE FORESTRY INITIATIVE Certified Sourcing
www.sfiprogram.org
SFI-00993
This Label Applies to Text Stock Only

Visit the official *Star Wars* website at: www.starwars.com.

CONTENTS

A long time ago in a galaxy far, far away. . . .

STAR WARS

THE PHANTOM MENACE

RACE TO THE FINISH LINE

A long time ago, on a small planet called Tatooine, a young boy named Anakin Skywalker looked up at the planet's moons. Although he had never left his home, Anakin had always dreamed of going on great adventures and racing across the stars.

One day, it looked like Anakin's dreams were coming true. He had met a Jedi Knight named Qui-Gon who needed supplies to repair his ship. Anakin didn't have money to help the Jedi, so he had entered a podrace, hoping to win the supplies.

Although Anakin had never won a race before, he knew that he could do it.

As the timer counted down to the beginning of the race, Anakin looked at all the other racers. He wasn't worried about any of them—except Sebulba. Anakin knew that Sebulba cheated to win. But he wouldn't get away with it this time!

Suddenly, the starting gong rang. They were off!

But something was wrong . . . Anakin's podracer wouldn't move!

Anakin began to panic. Sebulba must have done something to his podracer! But Anakin thought of what Qui-Gon had told him right before the race began: *Concentrate on the moment. Feel. Don't think. Use your instincts.*

Anakin took a deep breath, flipped a few switches, and restarted his engines. They roared to life, and Anakin quickly flew away. But he was a long way behind Sebulba.

Meanwhile, Sebulba knocked his ship against another racer's. The podracer crashed off the course and burst into flames! Sebulba laughed. One fewer racer to worry about!

Behind the crash, Anakin flew through a cavern and into a deep cave. One of the other racers wasn't paying attention and ran right into some rocks. The ship exploded! Anakin quickly flew around the fire.

That was close! Anakin thought.

Anakin raced through the stadium. He had two more laps to finish, but he smiled. He was catching up to Sebulba!

The racers thundered across the planet. Sebulba was still ahead of everyone else, but he wanted to make sure it stayed that way. Sebulba threw a piece of metal behind him, and it went right into another racer's engine! The engine exploded, and pieces of the podracer flew everywhere.

A piece cut through the cable connecting Anakin's cockpit to one of his engines. Anakin began to spin out of control! But he remembered Qui-Gon's words. Anakin couldn't just *worry* about his problem if he wanted to win the race. He needed to fix it.

Anakin quickly brought his cockpit under control and grabbed the loose cable. Soon he had reattached the engine and was back in the race! Sebulba and Anakin zoomed through the stadium one last time before the final lap. With all the other racers far behind, Anakin realized that Sebulba was the only one between him and the finish line.

Sebulba's podracer was much bigger than Anakin's. He forced
Anakin off the course and high up onto a cliff! But Anakin wasn't going
to be beaten. He changed gears and crashed back onto the course right
in front of Sebulba. For the first time, Anakin was in the lead!

Suddenly, Anakin saw smoke coming out of one of his engines. His podracer was on fire! The hard landing must have damaged it.

As Sebulba raced ahead of him, Anakin knew he didn't have a lot of time. He needed to fix his podracer—right away. Anakin closed a flap above the engine to put out the fire. Then he quickly pumped coolant into the overheated area. Soon the engine roared back to full power.

Anakin grinned. It was time to win the race.

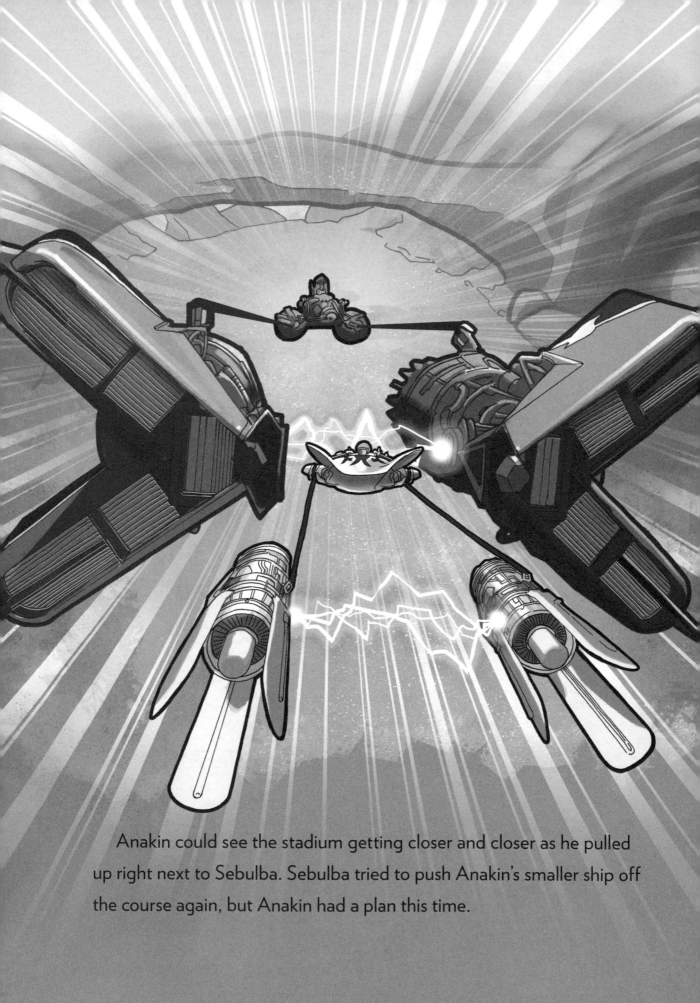

Anakin could see the stadium getting closer and closer as he pulled up right next to Sebulba. Sebulba tried to push Anakin's smaller ship off the course again, but Anakin had a plan this time.

As Sebulba rammed him, Anakin caught his podracer on Sebulba's. Sebulba was stuck! Then, as Sebulba tried to pull his ship away, Anakin unhooked their crafts. Sebulba zoomed wildly off course and smashed part of his podracer into a rock. Anakin had used Sebulba's own attack against him!

Anakin raised his hands over his head as he crossed the finish line. The crowd cheered. Qui-Gon ran to Anakin's podracer and lifted him high up onto his shoulders. Anakin had done what had seemed impossible. He had won the race!

Anakin smiled. One of his dreams had come true! He couldn't help wondering what great adventure he'd have next.

STAR WARS

ATTACK OF THE CLONES

YODA AND THE COUNT

Jedi Master Yoda was one of the leaders of the Jedi Order. He was wise and knew many things. Above all, Yoda believed in the Force. But now Yoda sensed a great disturbance in the Force. Count Dooku, Yoda's old apprentice, was trying to raise an army against Yoda and the other Jedi Knights!

The Jedi's search for Dooku led them to the planet Geonosis. A great battle broke out, and Dooku tried to escape. But Yoda's companions, Obi-Wan Kenobi and Anakin Skywalker, raced after him. Yoda sensed the presence of his powerful old apprentice and followed the two young Jedi to a small hangar bay far away from the battle.

When Yoda entered the hangar, he
saw Obi-Wan and Anakin hurt and on
the ground. Standing over them was the
evil Count Dooku!

Count Dooku glared at the Jedi. "Master Yoda," he said.

"Count Dooku," Yoda said. He knew that he had to stop Dooku to protect his two friends. He also knew that there was still a chance to stop the battle on Geonosis before it became a war.

"You have interfered with our affairs for the last time!" Dooku said as he used the Force to rip objects off the walls, then throw them straight at Yoda.

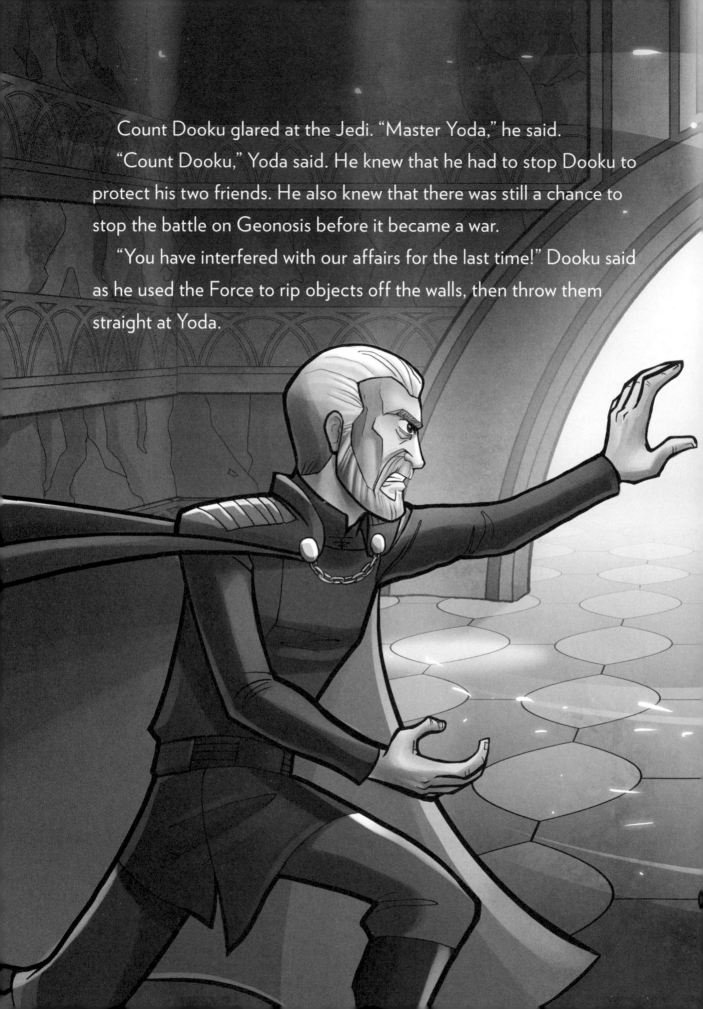

But Yoda knew Dooku's tricks and was prepared. He used the Force to swat Dooku's missiles aside. Frustrated, Dooku tried to bring the ceiling down on the small Jedi Master, but Yoda was too strong for him. He pushed the rocks away.

"Powerful you have become, Dooku," Master Yoda told the Count.

"I have become more powerful than any Jedi. Even you," Dooku replied. With that, the Count raised his hand and shot Force lightning at his old Jedi Master!

But Yoda refused to be afraid. He used the Force to bend the lightning up and away from him. Count Dooku could only watch in astonishment! He tried again, but this time Yoda closed his fist around the lightning until it disappeared!

"Much to learn you still have," Yoda told Count Dooku.

"It is obvious that this contest cannot be decided by our knowledge of the Force but by our skills with a lightsaber," the Count said as he raised his red lightsaber. Yoda called his own to his hand. Its green blade glowed as he lifted it to fight Count Dooku.

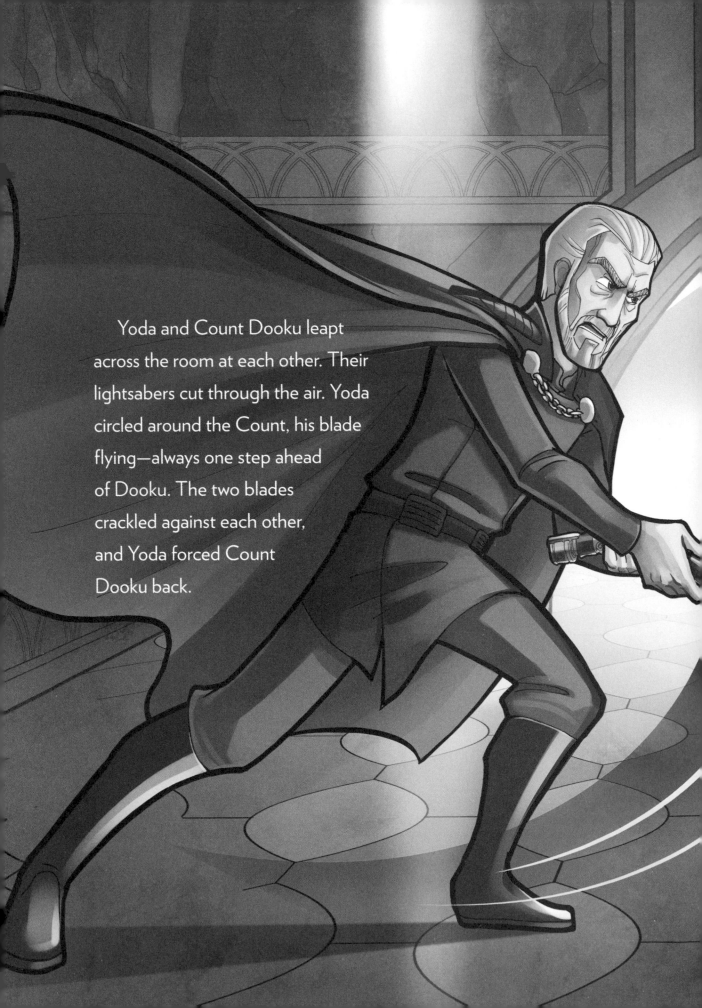

Yoda and Count Dooku leapt across the room at each other. Their lightsabers cut through the air. Yoda circled around the Count, his blade flying—always one step ahead of Dooku. The two blades crackled against each other, and Yoda forced Count Dooku back.

The Count was amazed as Yoda jumped high across the hangar to land smoothly back down in front of him. Dooku realized he wasn't powerful enough to beat Yoda.

"Fought well, you have, my old Padawan," Yoda told the Count.

"This is just the beginning," Dooku said. And then he smiled, because he had discovered a way to win the fight.

Count Dooku raised his hand, and a huge tower began to crash down toward the defenseless Obi-Wan and Anakin! Count Dooku gave Yoda the choice between capturing him and saving the lives of his fellow Jedi. For Yoda there was no choice. He dropped his lightsaber and raised both hands to stop the column from falling on his friends. He could sense Count Dooku escaping to his ship.

There was now no chance for peace, but Yoda trusted in the Force. Count Dooku thought that the dark side was a shortcut to victory, but Yoda knew that the Count's victory would not last long. The Force was more powerful than Dooku could even imagine, and with it Yoda and his friends would one day defeat the dark side.

STAR WARS

REVENGE OF THE SITH

THE LAST ADVENTURE

Obi-Wan Kenobi and Anakin Skywalker were a great team. Together, the two Jedi traveled across the galaxy and fought battles against the dark forces of the Sith. Their newest mission was to rescue Chancellor Palpatine, an important leader who had been kidnapped by Count Dooku and his cyborg henchman, General Grievous. Republic pilots fired on the evil general's battleship, giving Obi-Wan and Anakin the chance to sneak on board.

The two friends fought their way to the heart of the general's ship and found the Chancellor in a large room all by himself—or so the Jedi thought. "Count Dooku," Palpatine said, looking behind Obi-Wan and Anakin.

The friends turned around to see their nemesis, the Sith Lord Count Dooku, waiting for them.

"Get help. You're no match for him," the Chancellor ordered the two Jedi.

But Obi-Wan smiled. "Chancellor Palpatine, Sith Lords are our specialty," he said.

"You won't get away this time, Dooku," Obi-Wan said. But the Count didn't say anything. He just drew his lightsaber. The two Jedi lunged to attack the Sith Lord.

"I've been looking forward to this," Count Dooku said as Obi-Wan's and Anakin's blue lightsabers clashed against his threatening red blade.

"My powers have doubled since the last time we met, Count," Anakin said, clenching his fist.

"Good. Twice the pride, double the fall," Count Dooku said.

Anakin tried to surprise the Count from behind, but Dooku was expecting a trick. Count Dooku kicked Anakin and knocked him to the ground. Anakin watched in shock as Dooku used the Force to choke Obi-Wan and throw the Jedi Master to the ground, as well. Obi-Wan didn't move.

Anakin cried out in anger. He ran at the Count and fought as he had never fought before. Dooku was no match for Anakin's fury. Using the Count's own lightsaber, the young Jedi soon defeated the evil Sith Lord.

Anakin rushed to Obi-Wan, who was still unconscious on the floor.

"Leave him," the freed Chancellor said, "or we'll never make it."

But Anakin would never leave his friend behind. He picked up Obi-Wan and carried him across his back. As the ship rocked from an explosion, Anakin led the Chancellor to the elevators. It was time to finish the mission and escape General Grievous's ship before it was destroyed.

Before too long, Obi-Wan was awake and the two Jedi were almost at the hangar bay, where their faithful droid, R2-D2, was waiting to take them home. But General Grievous was one step ahead of the Jedi this time. He activated a ray shield around Anakin, Obi-Wan, and the Chancellor. They were trapped!

"Wait a minute. How did this happen? We're smarter than this," Obi-Wan said, thinking back to all the adventures he and Anakin had been on together. Well . . . maybe they had been trapped a few times.

"Apparently not," Anakin replied.

The two friends, Chancellor Palpatine, and the droid, R2-D2, were led before the evil General Grievous on his command deck. "That wasn't much of a rescue," the cyborg general said. He took the Jedi's weapons from them. "Your lightsabers will make a fine addition to my collection."

But Obi-Wan only smiled. "Not this time. And this time you won't escape," he said.

"Artoo!" Anakin cried. The droid beeped, and sparks flew as the droid created just the distraction the Jedi needed to free themselves and get their lightsabers back.

"Crush them!" General Grievous cried as his army of droids tried to stop the Jedi. But Anakin and Obi-Wan were a perfect team. Working together, the two Jedi soon took down all their enemies on the command deck—all except for General Grievous.

"You lose!" General Grievous yelled. He threw a staff into the front window of the command deck. The window shattered, and Anakin and Obi-Wan rushed to grab on to something before they were sucked into space. They could only watch as General Grievous leapt out the window. The general used his cyborg abilities to walk around the outside of the ship and into an escape pod. By the time the force fields came on, he was long gone.

Suddenly, there was a great explosion! The Chancellor almost fell over as Obi-Wan and Anakin looked at each other. They had taken too long. The ship was going to fall apart!

Anakin looked at the control panel. All the escape pods had been launched. They were stuck.

"Can you fly a cruiser like this?" Obi-Wan asked Anakin.

"Strap yourselves in," Anakin said as he took control of the ship. He didn't know if he could fly such a big ship, but he knew he had to try!

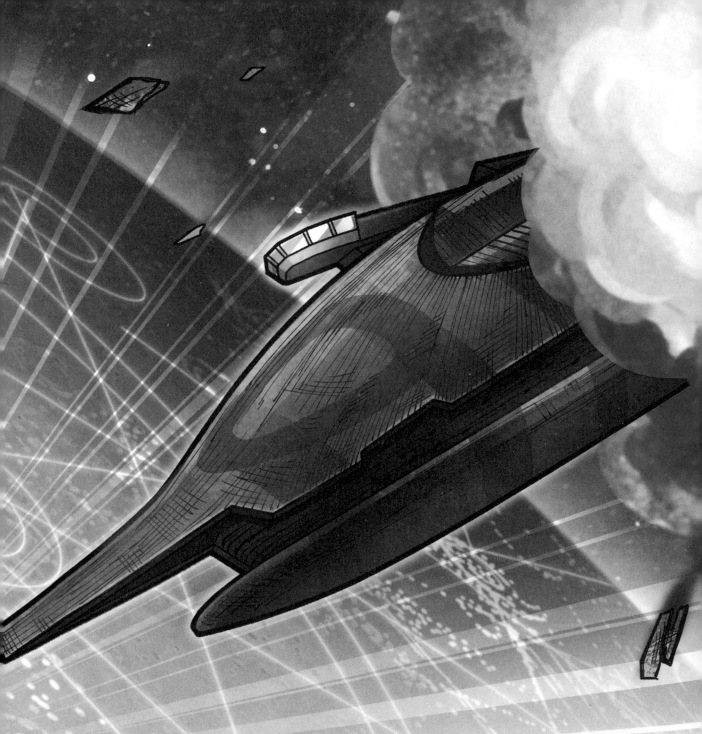

Anakin knew he was going to have to land the ship on the planet's surface. But as it got closer and closer to the planet's atmosphere, it began to break apart. R2-D2 beeped in alarm as the entire ship split in two!

"We lost something," Anakin told Obi-Wan.

"Not to worry. We are still flying half a ship," Obi-Wan replied.

Obi-Wan was right to trust his friend. The ship soon reached the planet's atmosphere, and Anakin maneuvered the broken vessel to hit the landing strip just right. With a crash the ship hit the ground and slid to a stop. They were safe!

"Another happy landing," Obi-Wan said with a smile.

With the Chancellor safe, Obi-Wan and Anakin had successfully completed another mission. Now it was time to get back to the Jedi Temple. Obi-Wan was sure there was already another mission waiting for them. But he also knew that, together, he and Anakin would be ready for anything.

STAR WARS

A NEW HOPE

ESCAPE FROM DARTH VADER

It was a time of war. Rebel spies fought the sinister Empire for control of the galaxy.

One of the rebels was named Princess Leia. She had been given plans for the Empire's newest weapon—the Death Star. Now Leia was on her starship, heading home to Alderaan. But she was not alone. An Imperial ship was chasing her!

On board Leia's ship were two droids: R2-D2 and C-3PO.

C-3PO was worried. He did not like being attacked!

"We're doomed," he said as the starship shook. "There'll be no escape for the princess this time!"

Suddenly, a loud blast rocked the ship. It had been captured! As the droids watched, the starship's main door blasted open. Stormtroopers rushed through, swarming the ship.

The stormtroopers fired their blasters at the rebels, and the rebels fired back. One by one the rebels fell. Soon the stormtroopers were in full control of the ship.

As the battle wound down, a mysterious figure emerged from the smoke. It was Darth Vader.

In the commotion, R2-D2 slipped away. Noticing that R2-D2 was missing, C-3PO set out to find his friend. "Artoo-Detoo, where are you?" he called.

Elsewhere on the ship, Princess Leia looked at the plans for the Death Star. She knew she had to keep them safe. If the Empire got the plans back, the rebels wouldn't stand a chance!

Just then, R2-D2 appeared. That gave Princess Leia an idea.

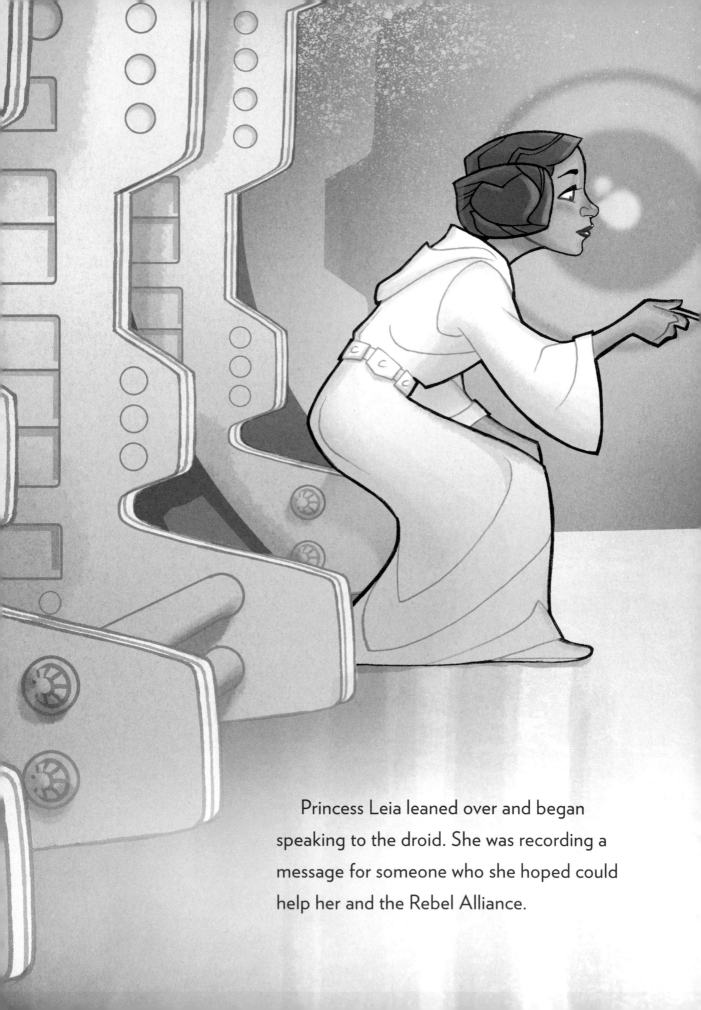

Princess Leia leaned over and began
speaking to the droid. She was recording a
message for someone who she hoped could
help her and the Rebel Alliance.

"I have placed information vital to the survival of the Rebellion into the memory systems of this Artoo unit," she explained.

When Princess Leia was done with her message, she inserted the plans for the Death Star into R2-D2. Then she told him where to go.

Princess Leia was just finishing her instructions when C-3PO found R2-D2.

"At last," he said. "Where have you been?" C-3PO pointed back at the stormtroopers. "They're heading in this direction. What are we going to do?"

But R2-D2 wasn't listening. He turned around and zipped off toward the escape pods.

Princess Leia watched until she was sure R2-D2 was safe. Then, lifting her hood over her head, she crept into the shadows. There was still a chance she could get away, too!

Meanwhile, Darth Vader was speaking to one of his commanders. "The Death Star plans are not in the main computer," the commander reported.

That did not make Darth Vader happy. "Tear this ship apart until you've found those plans," he ordered. "And bring me the passengers!"

The stormtroopers wasted no time. They had not been searching long before they spotted Princess Leia. She tried to escape, but she was not fast enough.

The troopers brought the princess to Darth Vader.

"I want to know what happened to the plans," he told her.

Princess Leia refused to speak. Darth Vader ordered his commander to take her away. He would get the truth out of her—somehow.

But the plans—and R2-D2—were about to leave the ship. They were inside an escape pod.

"You're not permitted in there," C-3PO told him. "It is restricted. You'll be deactivated for sure!"

R2-D2 just beeped at him.

"Secret mission?" C-3PO asked. "What plans? I'm not getting in there!"

Just then, another explosion
rocked the ship.

C-3PO hurried into the pod.
"I'm going to regret this," he said.

The door slammed, and the
escape pod rocketed off into space.

A short while later, the pod landed on a desert planet named Tatooine.

The plans were safe, but the droids' adventures were just beginning.

STAR WARS

A NEW HOPE

DESTROY THE DEATH STAR!

For years the Rebellion had struggled against the evil Galactic Empire. Now, for the first time, the rebels had an advantage. They had discovered a weakness in the Empire's greatest weapon—the Death Star.

"They could use a good pilot like you," Luke Skywalker said to his friend Han Solo as the Rebels prepared for their attack.

"Sorry, kid," Han said. The smuggler wasn't interested. He had more important things to do.

Luke walked away disappointed. But he needed to keep his mind on the mission. At times like this, he missed his old teacher, Obi-Wan Kenobi.

Luke climbed into the cockpit of his X-wing while they loaded his astromech droid, R2-D2, into the ship. Luke was glad the little droid was his copilot. The two friends had been through a lot together.

The fleet of X-wings flew toward the space station.

"Look at the size of that thing," one of the pilots said. As they approached the massive Death Star, everyone started to get nervous.

Luke heard a mysterious voice inside his head: *Luke, the Force will be with you. . . .*

Soon the Death Star's cannons began to shoot at the X-wings. Laser fire exploded all around Luke and his friends. But there was no time for hesitation.

"I'm going in," said Luke.

Luke heard the voice again: *Luke, trust your feelings.* The voice seemed familiar, and it helped Luke focus.

He dodged the laser fire and swooped toward the surface of the Death Star with the other X-wings.

But the X-wings were not alone. A fleet of TIE fighters appeared behind them. That was going to make things even more difficult—especially since Darth Vader himself was leading the enemy ships.

The TIE fighters fired on the X-wings. Luke's ship was shot! "I'm hit, but not bad," Luke told the other pilots. "Artoo, see what you can do back there." R2-D2 got to work fixing the damage. The little droid was both brave and smart.

The first of the X-wings entered the Death Star's trench. The lead pilot got close to the exhaust port—the one weakness of the giant space station.

The pilot fired . . . but he missed!

Back at the rebel base, Princess Leia and C-3PO were worried about their friends. But they were also worried about the Death Star. If it got too close to the base, it would destroy them all.

The second attack run of rebel ships dove into the canyon to take their shot. But they missed, too! It was all up to Luke. He just had to dodge Darth Vader and the enemy TIE fighters on his tail.

Luke tried to use the targeting computer to make the shot. But he heard the familiar voice in his head again: *Use the Force, Luke*. It was Obi-Wan!

Luke shut off the computer and trusted himself. Right as he was about to take his shot, Darth Vader's TIE fighter appeared behind him.

Darth Vader's lasers locked on to Luke's X-wing. "I have you now," Vader said triumphantly.

But before Vader could fire, another ship swooped in and shot all the TIE fighters. It was Han Solo in the *Millennium Falcon*! He had returned just in time to save his friend.

"*Yahoo!*" Han shouted with excitement. Then he added, "You're all clear, kid. Now let's blow this thing and go home!"

Luke was so happy his friend had joined the fight after all.

But everything still rested on Luke's shoulders. If he didn't make the shot, the rebels were doomed. Luke thought about what Obi-Wan had said.

Luke closed his eyes and used the Force. He waited . . . then, when the moment was right, he fired.

Luke did it! The torpedoes flew into the exhaust port. "Great shot, kid," Han Solo said. "That was one in a million!"

The rebel ships sped away from the Death Star as fast as they could.

Seconds later, the entire space station exploded in a giant burst of light! The Death Star had been destroyed.

As Luke and his friends flew to safety, he heard Obi-Wan's voice in his head one last time. *Remember, the Force will be with you. Always.*

Luke smiled to himself. He and his friends had defeated the Empire and rescued the rebels. And soon they would save the entire galaxy.

STAR WARS

THE EMPIRE STRIKES BACK

THE BATTLE OF HOTH

Deep in the cold reaches of space, the ice planet Hoth orbited a pale sun. The surface of the planet was a frozen wasteland. Nobody lived there.

At least . . . nobody was *supposed* to live there. And that made Hoth the perfect place for the Rebel Alliance to hide from the evil Empire.

From the helm of his Imperial Star Destroyer, Darth Vader stared grimly out into space. He was looking everywhere for the Rebel Alliance. Vader sent hundreds of probe droids into space, seeking any sign of the rebels.

Soon the rebels noticed a droid snooping around their base on Hoth. Princess Leia hurried to the command center with Han Solo and his friend Chewbacca to discuss the droid.

"Come on, Chewie," Han told his Wookiee copilot. "Let's check it out."

The droid self-destructed before Han could capture it. But first it sent a signal back to Darth Vader. The secret rebel base wasn't a secret anymore.

"It's a good bet the Empire knows we're here," Han told Leia.

Darth Vader wasted no time. His fleet left for the Hoth system right away. They didn't want to give the rebels a chance to escape.

While Vader's Star Destroyers lay in wait in the sky above Hoth, four armored Imperial walkers began to make their way across the icy tundra toward the rebel base.

Princess Leia ordered the evacuation of the base. Most of the rebels hurried onto transport ships and left immediately. But others remained on Hoth to stand and fight. They would protect the base until everyone else had escaped. Leia stayed with them; she didn't want to leave her troops alone.

Han Solo stayed with Leia . . . he didn't want to leave *her* alone.

Meanwhile, Luke Skywalker climbed into a snowspeeder and led a squadron of fighter pilots out onto the plains of Hoth. They were going to try to fend off the monstrous Imperial walkers. Luke hoped to keep them far away from the base.

And far away from his friends Leia and Han.

Luke's squadron tried firing directly at the walkers, but it did no good. "That armor's too strong for blasters," Luke declared. So they used cables instead, tangling one of the walker's legs together.

It worked!

Luke ran underneath another walker. He fired a grappling hook into its belly and pulled himself up underneath it. Then he used his Jedi lightsaber to cut it open.

Luke threw a grenade into the walker and dropped back to the
ground. *Boom!* The walker flashed with green sparks and exploded.

But even as Luke tried to keep the walkers away, the base was taking fire. The floor shook violently. Han and Leia could barely stand up! Then the alert came:

"Imperial troops have entered the base."

Han grabbed Leia's hand. "Come on," he said. "That's it." It was time to go.

Han and Leia ran to Han's ship, the *Millennium Falcon*. The golden droid C-3PO followed on their heels.

Darth Vader personally led his Imperial troops into the now-empty rebel base. As the troops searched for any signs of life, Chewie and Han tried to get the *Millennium Falcon* started. The engine revved, then choked. Steam billowed everywhere.

"Would it help if I got out and pushed?" Leia said sarcastically.

"It might!" snapped Han.

Han and Chewie worked furiously to get the ship running. Leia scowled. They were going to be captured by the Empire unless they could get the *Millennium Falcon*'s engine started.

Just as Han and Chewie were making their final repairs, Darth Vader
and a group of Imperial snowtroopers entered the hangar where the
Millennium Falcon was docked. They opened fire on the ship.

Han and Chewie fired back as the engine rumbled to life.

"See?" Han said.

Leia rolled her eyes.

"Someday you're going to be wrong," Leia told Han as the ship leapt into the air and rocketed out of the base. "And I just hope I'm there to see it."

Darth Vader watched angrily as the ship escaped into the sky.

Luke Skywalker watched them go, as well. He knew that the *Millennium Falcon* was the last ship to leave the base. Luke had done his job, and Han and Leia had gotten away.

The Rebel Alliance was safe once again.

STAR WARS

THE EMPIRE STRIKES BACK

A JEDI, YOU MUST BECOME

Luke Skywalker would become one of the greatest Jedi Knights in the galaxy. But he wasn't always a powerful Jedi. In the beginning, he was just a boy—no different from any other.

Luke fought bravely as a pilot for the Rebellion. He even destroyed the Death Star! But Luke decided that he could best help the rebels if he trained to become a Jedi Knight.

In a vision, Luke's old friend Obi-Wan Kenobi said to him, *You will go to the Dagobah system. There you will learn from Yoda, the Jedi Master who instructed me.* Luke knew that Obi-Wan would appear to him only if his message was very important. Luke and his droid, R2-D2, flew to Dagobah right away.

Dagobah was not what Luke had expected. He thought a Jedi Master would live on a beautiful, serene world—but that was not what Dagobah was like at all!

The planet was wet, muggy, and crawling with bugs, critters, and wild animals. It could be summed up with one word—*gross*!

When Luke landed, his X-wing fighter sank right into the marsh water.

Suddenly, Luke felt someone watching him and he spun around, pulling out his blaster. Standing in front of Luke was a pale green creature with big pointy ears.

"I am wondering, why are you here?" the creature asked.

"I'm looking for a great warrior," Luke replied.

The creature shook his head. "A great warrior? Wars not make one great."

Luke had to admit the creature had a point. "I'm looking for a Jedi Master," he explained.

"Ohhhhh. Jedi Master," the creature said. "Yoda. You seek Yoda."

The creature promised to take Luke to Yoda. But first the creature stopped at his home and fed Luke dinner.

With no sign of Yoda anywhere, Luke grew impatient. "We're wasting our time!"

The creature turned away from Luke. "I cannot teach him. The boy has no patience. . . . He is not ready."

Luke suddenly realized that this was no ordinary creature. "Yoda!"

Yoda laughed at Luke. "Adventure—heh. Excitement—heh. A Jedi craves not these things. You are reckless."

Luke told Yoda that he had learned so much already and he was not afraid. Finally, Yoda agreed to train him.

Luke's first test was to run through a swampy obstacle course.

As Luke trained his body, Yoda helped him develop his mind.

"A Jedi uses the Force for knowledge and defense," Yoda said, "never for attack."

Luke began to understand that being a Jedi was less about him and more about helping others.

Luke also learned to move objects with the Force. One day, Luke stacked a tower of rocks with his mind—while standing on his head! But as Luke placed the final rock, his X-wing began to sink deeper into the swamp. Luke lost his concentration and fell to the ground with a thud.

Thinking about trying to raise his ship from the muck, Luke said to Yoda, "Moving stones around is one thing, but this is totally different."

"No, no different. You must unlearn what you have learned." Yoda said.

Luke concentrated again. He knew that he would one day have to confront Darth Vader, the powerful Sith Lord. He needed to be as strong in the Force as possible.

Luke turned back to the sunken X-wing and said, "All right, I'll give it a try. . . ."

Yoda stopped Luke, saying, "Do. Or do not. There is no try."

Luke concentrated on Yoda's words and lessons, letting the Force flow through him.

Slowly, the X-wing began to rise. Luke was as surprised as R2-D2 was excited. The little droid exclaimed with his own brand of beeps and whistles.

But Luke struggled with his doubts. He knew that an X-wing was very heavy. How could he possibly manage to lift it? Slowly, the ship sank back into the swamp.

Luke was sad and discouraged. "I can't. It's too big."

"Size matters not," Yoda said. "Look at me. Judge me by my size, do you?"

Yoda reached out with his tiny old hand, and the ship began to move!

Yoda concentrated even more and the ship floated through the air until it came to rest on solid ground.

"I don't believe it," Luke said, astonished.

"That," Yoda replied, "is why you fail."

Luke continued his training, more determined than ever. One day, Luke saw a vision through the Force. He saw his friends Han Solo and Princess Leia—and they were in trouble! They had been captured by Darth Vader.

"It is the future you see," Yoda explained.

"I've got to go to them," Luke insisted. He couldn't bear to think that Han and Leia were in danger.

Luke knew that a Jedi Knight was a defender, not an attacker. He acted out of protection rather than anger. It was a Jedi Knight's duty to put other people ahead of himself. Luke felt that he had come far enough in his Jedi training to make his own decisions.

Luke decided to put his training on hold and go rescue his friends. "I'll return," he told Yoda. "I promise."

As Luke's ship took flight, Yoda wished that he had more time to help Luke prepare. Luke's battles would not be easy, but he was good at heart. No matter where he went, the Force would be with him, always.

STAR WARS

RETURN OF THE JEDI

RESCUE FROM JABBA'S PALACE

Han Solo was in trouble. He had been captured by Darth Vader and frozen in carbonite. The Sith Lord had then given Solo to the bounty hunter Boba Fett.

Now the frozen hero was in the one place he had desperately been trying to avoid: the palace of Jabba the Hutt.

Luke Skywalker had a plan to rescue Han. He sent R2-D2 and C-3PO to Jabba with a holographic message.

"Greetings, Exalted One," Luke said. "I seek an audience with Your Greatness to bargain for Solo's life. As a token of my goodwill, I present to you a gift: these two droids."

Jabba looked at R2-D2 and C-3PO and laughed. "There will be no bargain," he said. "I will not give up my favorite decoration."

Jabba was not about to give up the droids, either. C-3PO was assigned to work as a translator in the palace, and R2-D2 was sent to Jabba's sail barge.

Later that night, as Jabba celebrated his victory over Han, a bounty hunter interrupted the party.

C-3PO couldn't believe what he was seeing. The hunter had captured Chewbacca, the Wookiee!

Jabba was thrilled. He and the bounty hunter agreed on a price for Chewbacca, and Chewie was sent to the dungeon.

But this was no ordinary bounty hunter. It was Princess Leia in disguise!

That night, while everyone slept, she crept through Jabba's palace and freed Han from the carbonite.

"I've got to get you out of here," Leia said.

As she helped Han to his feet, an evil laugh filled the room. It was Jabba! His servants took hold of the weakened Han and threw him in the dungeon with Chewie.

Jabba kept Leia as a servant in his throne room.

The next day, a mysterious visitor arrived. It was Luke.

Using his Jedi powers, he tried to trick Jabba into freeing his friends. "You will bring Captain Solo and the Wookiee to me," Luke said. "I warn you not to underestimate my powers."

"There will be no bargain, young Jedi," Jabba replied. "I shall enjoy watching you die."

The floor opened beneath Luke, and he fell into a dark, musty pit.

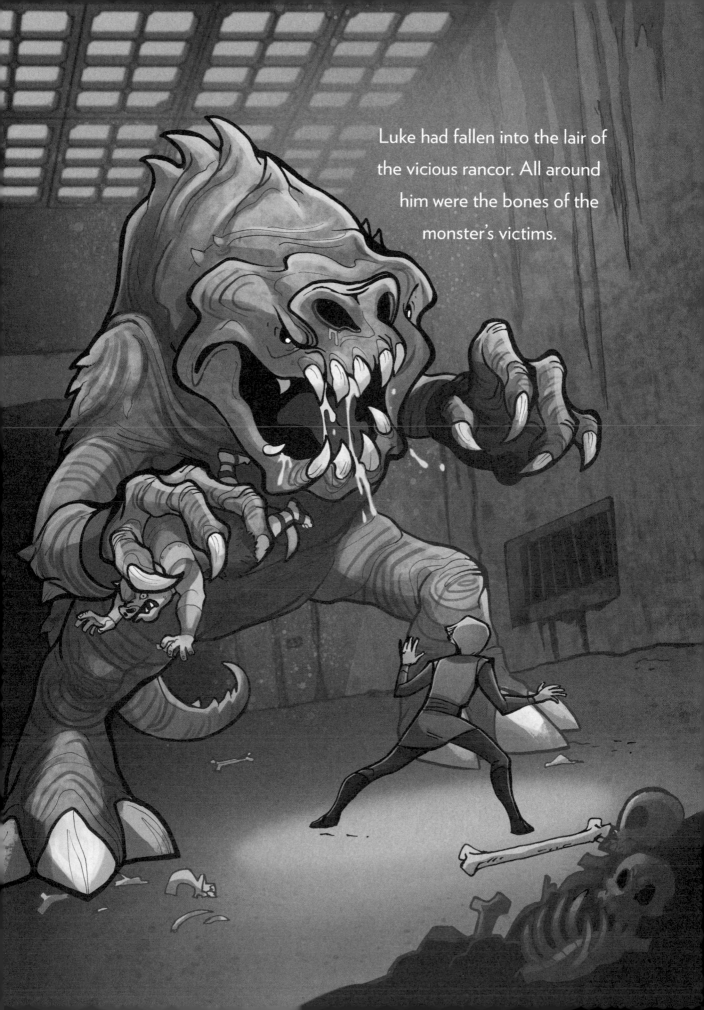

Luke had fallen into the lair of the vicious rancor. All around him were the bones of the monster's victims.

Suddenly, a gate opened and the rancor slithered into the pit. The beast picked Luke up in one hand and opened its giant mouth. But Luke was ready! He shoved a bone between the rancor's teeth so it couldn't bite down.

Then, rushing past the beast, he threw a boulder at the gate's controls. The gate slammed down, crushing the rancor.

Jabba was not happy. He had expected his monster to defeat the Jedi!

At Jabba's order, Luke, Han, and Chewie were brought before him.

"Jabba the Hutt has decreed that you are to be terminated . . . immediately," C-3PO translated. "You will be taken to the Dune Sea and cast into the Pit of Carkoon, the nesting place of the all-powerful Sarlacc."

As Jabba's servants seized the three prisoners, Luke looked back at Jabba over his shoulder. "You should have bargained," he said. "That's the last mistake you'll ever make."

On board Jabba's sail barge, R2-D2 slipped away from the crowd. He watched from the window as Jabba's guards prepared the prisoners. One of the guards was Lando in disguise!

Luke stepped onto the plank over the Sarlacc pit. With a nod to R2-D2, he jumped!

Suddenly, R2-D2 shot an object into the sky. Luke grabbed the plank
and sprang back onto the deck of Jabba's ship. Reaching out his hand,
he took hold of the object R2-D2 had thrown.

It was Luke's lightsaber!

Luke, Han, and Chewie wasted no time. The three jumped into
battle with Jabba's men, hurling them overboard and into the mouth of
the Sarlacc.

Inside Jabba's barge, Princess Leia seized her moment to escape.
Wrapping her chains around the evil gangster, she defeated him once
and for all.

R2-D2 zapped Leia's chains and freed her.

While Luke fought off the rest of Jabba's men, Leia aimed the barge cannon at the deck. Then, holding on to each other, Luke and Leia swung to safety.

Reunited at last, the group soared across the desert of Tatooine. Behind them, Jabba's barge exploded.

They had defeated him. But more important, they had rescued Han. They were a team again.

STAR WARS

RETURN OF THE JEDI

THE EWOKS JOIN THE FIGHT

Han Solo was on a special mission on the forest moon of Endor. He had landed there with Princess Leia, Luke Skywalker, Chewbacca, R2-D2, and C-3PO. The rebels were looking for a secret bunker that hid a special machine—a machine that could help them destroy the Death Star!

As the rebels snuck through the forest, they spotted two biker scouts. The scouts patrolled the forest and guarded the bunker.

"Chewie and I will take care of this," Han said, pointing to the scouts. "You stay here."

But as Han and Chewie attacked, more scouts appeared.

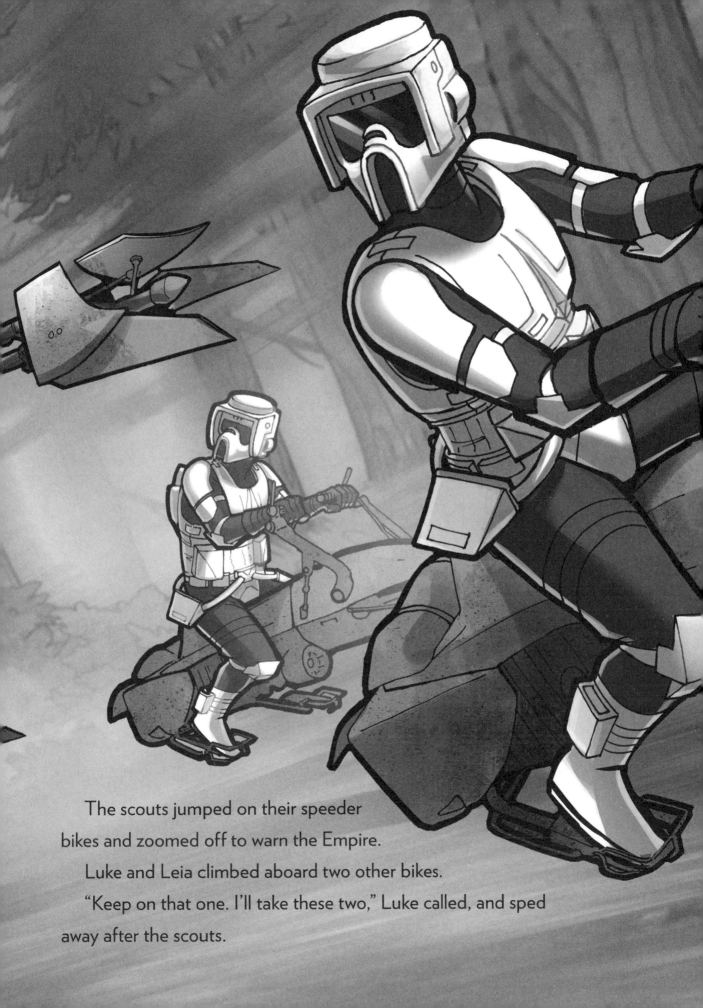

The scouts jumped on their speeder
bikes and zoomed off to warn the Empire.

Luke and Leia climbed aboard two other bikes.

"Keep on that one. I'll take these two," Luke called, and sped

away after the scouts.

Leia chased after the other scout. She managed to catch up to him, but then the scout fired his blaster at her. Leia tried to dodge the blast and rolled off her speeder.

She was all alone in the forest, with no way to get back to her friends.

Suddenly, a small furry creature appeared. It was an Ewok. He poked at Leia with a sharp stick.

"Cut it out," Leia said, standing up and brushing herself off.

Leia sighed and looked down at the Ewok again. "Maybe you can help me," she said. But the Ewok seemed afraid of her.

"I won't hurt you," Leia said. "Here. Want something to eat?"

The Ewok was just getting comfortable with Leia when a biker scout appeared behind her! The Ewok quickly hid behind a log.

"Freeze!" the scout said.

Using a large stick, the hidden Ewok hit the trooper. Together, Leia and the Ewok disarmed the scout.

"Come on. Let's get out of here," Leia said.

The Ewok took Leia's hand and led her toward his village.

Meanwhile, Luke and his friends searched the forest for Leia. But all they found was a wrecked speeder and Princess Leia's helmet.

While they were looking for Leia, a group of Ewoks found *them*! The Ewoks did not seem happy about the strangers in their woods.

The Ewoks tied up the rebels and took them to their village.

When they arrived, the rebels were surprised to see Princess Leia!
Leia tried to tell the Ewoks that Han, Luke, and Chewie were her
friends, but they did not listen. Only C-3PO was allowed to remain free.
The Ewoks seemed to think he was a powerful being.

"Threepio," Luke said. "Tell them if they don't do as you wish, you'll
become angry and use your magic."

C-3PO did as Luke said, but the Ewoks still wouldn't listen.

Closing his eyes, Luke used the Force to make
C-3PO float.

The Ewoks were amazed. Now they *knew* the
droid was powerful. They quickly did as he said and
untied his friends.

That night, the Ewoks gathered around C-3PO, who told them tales of the rebels and Darth Vader.

The Ewoks liked the stories. And they liked the rebels.

They decided to make the rebels part of their tribe!

One of the Ewoks jumped up and began to hug Han. As he did so, he jabbered away. But Han couldn't understand what he was saying.

"He says the Ewoks are going to show us the quickest way to the shield generator," C-3PO translated.

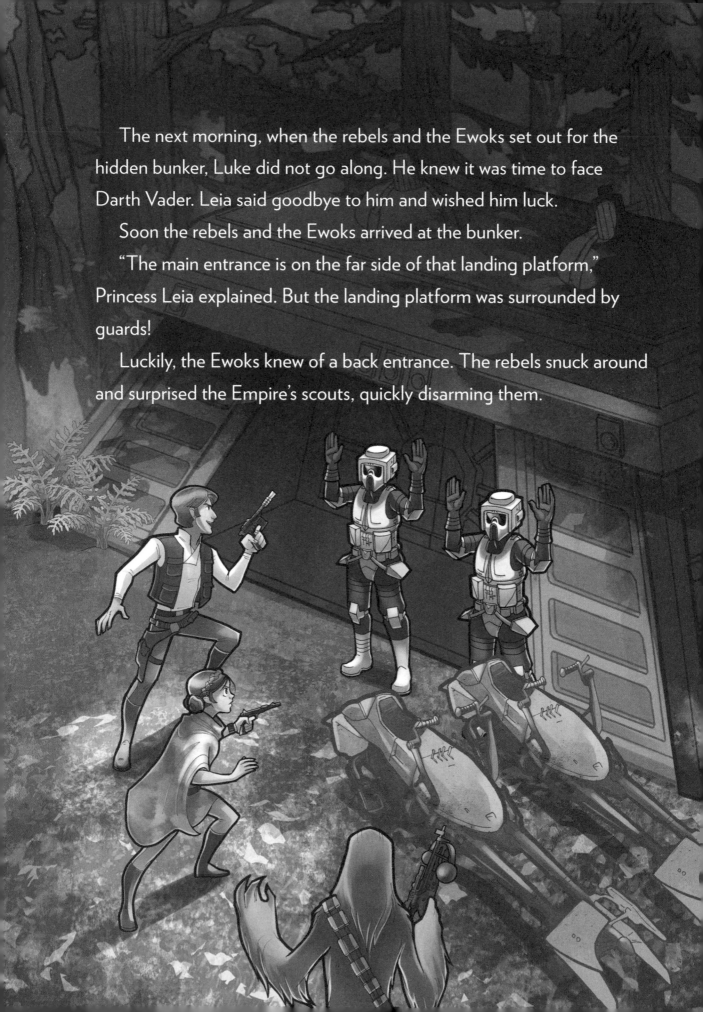

The next morning, when the rebels and the Ewoks set out for the hidden bunker, Luke did not go along. He knew it was time to face Darth Vader. Leia said goodbye to him and wished him luck.

Soon the rebels and the Ewoks arrived at the bunker.

"The main entrance is on the far side of that landing platform," Princess Leia explained. But the landing platform was surrounded by guards!

Luckily, the Ewoks knew of a back entrance. The rebels snuck around and surprised the Empire's scouts, quickly disarming them.

Han, Chewie, and Leia made their way deep inside the bunker. But before they could turn off the Death Star's shield generator, they were surrounded by Imperial soldiers. It was a trap! The Empire had been waiting for them.

From their hiding places in the forest, the Ewoks watched as Imperial stormtroopers and scouts marched Han, Leia, and Chewie back out of the bunker. The Ewoks knew they had to help their friends. Along with C-3PO, the Ewoks distracted the soldiers, drawing them away from Leia, Han, and Chewie.

The Ewoks knew just what to do.

They threw rocks at the stormtroopers.

They destroyed the Empire's machines.

They tripped the scouts and tied them up.

With the Empire's soldiers taken care of, Han Solo did what he had set out to do. He blew up the bunker! The Death Star was no longer protected.

Thanks to the Ewoks, the rebels could destroy the Death Star and defeat the Empire—once and for all.

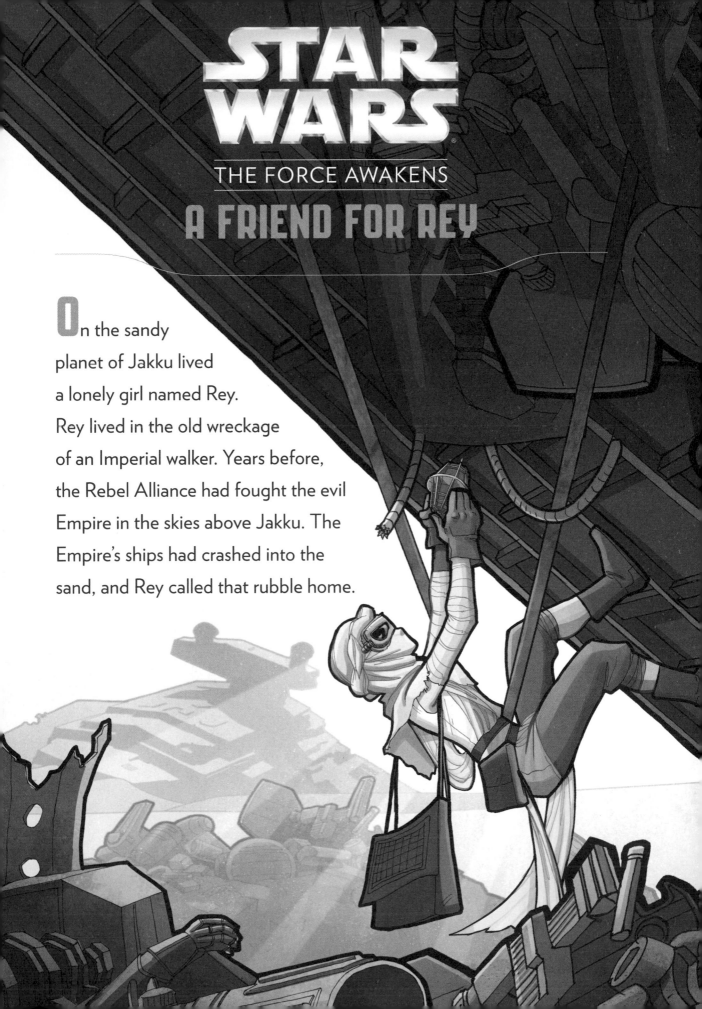

STAR WARS

THE FORCE AWAKENS

A FRIEND FOR REY

On the sandy planet of Jakku lived a lonely girl named Rey. Rey lived in the old wreckage of an Imperial walker. Years before, the Rebel Alliance had fought the evil Empire in the skies above Jakku. The Empire's ships had crashed into the sand, and Rey called that rubble home.

Rey searched the Empire's crashed ships to look for used parts. Rey could sell the parts to Unkar Plutt at Niima Outpost for food. Unkar was not always fair with his trades. But Rey made enough to get by.

One night Rey was eating the small dinner she had managed to get from Unkar by trading parts. Suddenly, she heard a beeping noise coming from outside. The beeping sounded . . . frightened? Rey ran toward the noise to see what was happening.

Rey saw an alien riding a scaly beast. The alien had trapped a little white-and-orange droid beneath a net, and the droid was beeping for help.

Rey called out to the alien to stop. She gripped her battle staff, ready to fight. But the alien just shouted angrily at Rey. She could tell he didn't want to fight her.

So Rey walked over to the droid and began cutting him out of the net.

The alien decided the droid wasn't worth the trouble. He rode away on his beast, still shouting insults at Rey.

The droid beeped questioningly.

"That's just a Teedo," Rey explained as the alien vanished in the distance. "Wants you for parts."

The droid thanked Rey for helping him and told her that his name was BB-8.

"Where'd you come from?" Rey asked the little droid.

But BB-8 refused to tell her. He said it was a secret.

"Really? Well, me too. Big secret," Rey teased. If BB-8 wanted to keep to himself, that was fine by her. She told him how to get to Niima Outpost, then started to leave.

But BB-8 followed her.

"You can't come with me," Rey said.

BB-8 beeped sadly. He did not want to be alone in the big desert.

Rey sighed. She told BB-8 he could stay with her for one night—and *only* one night.

BB-8 beeped with happiness and followed Rey all the way home.

The next morning, Rey took BB-8 to Niima Outpost.

"There's a trader in bay three, might be able to give you a lift wherever you're going."

Once again, Rey started to leave BB-8 behind, but he refused to let her go. He insisted he was waiting for his owner to find him on Jakku.

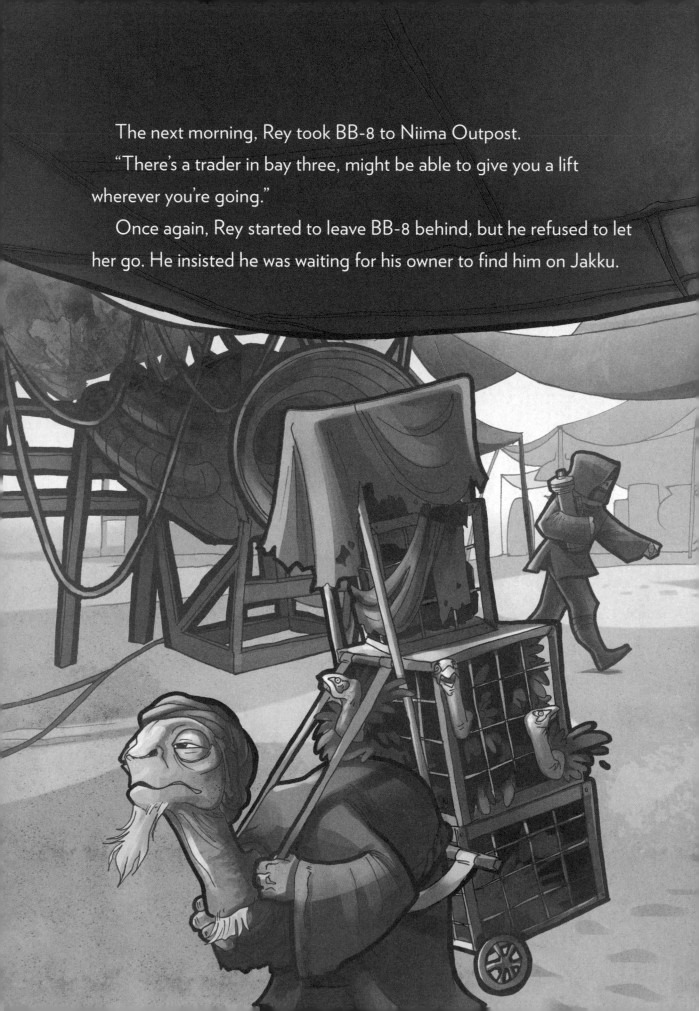

Rey let BB-8 follow her to Unkar's. There she traded all the spare parts she had found the previous day. Unkar also offered to buy BB-8. He said he would give her months' worth of food for the droid.

BB-8 beeped in worry. He did not like where this conversation was going!

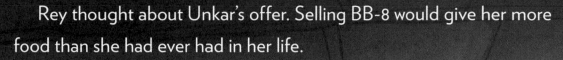

Rey thought about Unkar's offer. Selling BB-8 would give her more food than she had ever had in her life.

But as Rey looked at the little droid, she knew she could never sell him—no matter how much it would cost her.

"The droid is not for sale," Rey told Unkar.

Unkar was very angry. But Rey didn't care. Together, Rey and BB-8 left Unkar's shop behind them.

The pair walked side by side through the outpost, chatting happily.

Rey smiled to herself. She didn't know what her future held, but for now it was just nice to have a friend.

STAR WARS

THE FORCE AWAKENS

RATHTARS ON THE LOOSE!

The *Millennium Falcon* zoomed through the far reaches of space on an important mission.

Inside the *Falcon* were Rey, a young scavenger; Finn, a former stormtrooper; and BB-8, a small droid with a big secret. The three new friends were flying to the Resistance's base to help in the fight against the evil First Order.

But their flight was cut short when a giant cargo ship appeared above them and pulled the *Falcon* inside.

The three quickly hid as two figures climbed on board the *Falcon*.

It was a human and a Wookiee. The pair walked through the *Falcon*, examining the old ship. They seemed to know every corridor, every turn . . . and every hiding place! In no time at all, the man and the Wookiee found Finn, Rey, and BB-8.

"Where'd you get this ship?" the man asked. Rey explained that it had been left on Jakku, after it had been stolen many times.

"Well, Han Solo just stole back the *Millennium Falcon* for good!" the man said.

Rey couldn't believe her ears. Han Solo. *The* Han Solo!

Han had been a general in the Rebel Alliance. He and Chewbacca, the Wookiee, had helped Luke Skywalker, Princess Leia, and the rebels win the war against the evil Galactic Empire. They were heroes.

But Han was no longer a rebel general, and he wasn't part of the new Resistance. He just wanted Rey, Finn, and their droid off his ship.

"No!" Rey pleaded. "We have to get BB-8 to the Resistance base. He has information about Luke Skywalker."

Han stopped in surprise. Luke had been missing for years. But before Han could ask Rey anything more, there was a loud metallic *KA-CHUNK!* Han ordered everyone to hide in the cargo bay while he and Chewie investigated.

Two dangerous gangs—the Guavian Death Gang and the Kanjiklub Gang—had worked together to enter Han's cargo ship. Han owed money to both gangs, and they were there to collect.

It was a standoff, with Han and Chewie caught between two deadly enemies.

Han tried to talk his way out of a fight. "Guys. You're all gonna get what I promised. Have I ever not delivered before?"

"Twice," one of the gang leaders replied.

Rey and Finn could hear everything from their hiding place. They knew they had to help. "If we close the blast doors in that corridor, we can trap both gangs!" Rey said.

Quickly, Rey tried to rewire the door controls. But instead of closing the blast doors, she accidentally opened the doors to Han's cargo crates.

The lights flickered as a terrifying growl came from the open crates. Out slithered three rathtars—large creatures that looked like octopuses but crawled on land instead of underwater.

The rathtars attacked the gang members, giving Han and Chewie a chance to escape. They fought their way past many of the angry thugs. Han and Chewie wouldn't let anything or anyone stand in the way of their getting back to the *Falcon*.

Rey and Finn tried to get back to the *Falcon*, too. But one of the rathtars grabbed Finn and carried him off. Rey chased the beast through the cargo ship until she reached a control panel. Rey quickly flipped a few switches, and a large blast door closed directly on top of the creature. Finn was free!

As the battle raged on, Han and Chewie were getting closer and closer to the *Falcon*. But as they made their way toward the ship, Chewie got hit in the shoulder.

Han quickly grabbed Chewie's bowcaster and fired at the oncoming gang members. It worked! Han held them off long enough for everyone to get aboard the *Falcon*.

Han slid into the pilot seat as Finn helped Chewbacca to the medical bay. With Chewie hurt, Han would need someone to be his copilot. Rey quickly hopped into Chewie's seat.

"We're gonna jump to lightspeed," Han said.

"From inside the hangar? Is that even possible?" Rey asked.

"I never ask that question until after I've done it," was Han's only reply.

Han and Rey worked together to get the ship ready for lightspeed.

"Come on, baby, don't let me down!" Han said, then started the engines.

Nothing happened.

Rey figured out what was wrong right away and hit one more switch. "Compressor," she explained matter-of-factly.

Han tried the hyperdrive again, and the *Falcon* blasted away from the massive cargo ship. There was no way the gangs would catch them now!

As the *Falcon* flew through space, the group began to talk. Rey and Finn explained that BB-8 contained vital information that could help the Resistance and stop the First Order once and for all.

Han and Chewie agreed to fly them all to their destination. It felt right for the *Falcon* to be once again fighting an evil that threatened the galaxy. Together, they might even be able to defeat it.